This igloo book belongs to...

....

igloobooks

Published in 2020
First published in the UK by Igloo Books Ltd
An imprint of Igloo Books Ltd
Cottage Farm, NN6 0BJ, UK
Owned by Bonnier Books
Sveavägen 56, Stockholm, Sweden
www.igloobooks.com

1220 001
2 4 6 8 10 9 7 5 3 1
ISBN 978-1-83903-463-3

Written by Stephanie Moss
Illustrated by Lee Cosgrove

Designed and edited by Justine Ablett

Printed and manufactured in China

Uh-oh! It's the...
UNICORNS!

igloobooks

Dullsville is a boring place.
The town is dull and grey.
Nothing ever happens until,
suddenly, one day...

A rainbow **BURSTS** out from the clouds
and lights the gloomy sky.

A herd of unicorns appears,
but nobody knows why.

One says, "We've come to visit you and see all of the sights!"

They hop on board the bus and flash the grumpy driver's lights.

DULL01

They start snapping selfies all
around the grey town square.

They upset town hall meetings
and spin in the office chairs.

"These streets should be more fun,"
they say, and turn them into clouds.

They teach the pets new tricks to
make their boring owners proud.

The playground is deserted.
"Oh, we can't have this!" they cry.
So, they make a land of candy
and turn rainbows into slides.

"What is this?" the people ask.
"Our town isn't for you!
We like things the way they are.
Now keep out. Go on. SHOO!"

Unicorns don't give up, so do you think they stop there?

In the Dullsville salon, they transform everyone's hair!

"Have a sparkle latte and
try this cupcake surprise,"
says Twinkle, when she eats the
tasteless Dullsville café pies.

They disrupt swimming lessons,
as they make a lot of noise
and throw a great big splash party
with all the best pool toys.

Dullsville's taste in fashion
is as boring as can be.
But with some special magic,
they go on a shopping spree!

"Let's liven up this maths class,"
they say that afternoon.
So, they have a roller disco
throwing shapes to funky tunes.

The town has been turned upside down.
Dullsville is changed forever.

As everybody snoozes in their dreary homes that night,

the unicorns all creep inside to have a glitter fight!

A little girl speaks up. She says,

But they just want to play. You're all SUPER BORING and the unicorns should stay.

So, people look around.

They notice everything is bright!

At first, they just saw chaos.

Now they see a different sight.

People start to smile and
joy spreads across their face.
The unicorns have made
Dullsville a much happier place.

Children race into the streets. Their parents follow, too.

There are loads more awesome things for everyone to do!

The unicorns still visit as the years pass Dullsville by.

This time, people cheer when they swoop down from up high.

Everybody loves it when their new friends come to call.
Life with a bit of
SPARKLE
isn't so bad after all!